Rudyard Kipling's
JUST SO STORIES

How the
WHALE
Got His Throat

Retold and illustrated by

SHOO RAYNER

ORCHARD BOOKS

Long, long ago, at the very beginning of time, when everything was just getting sorted out, there was a Whale, and he ate fishes.

How the WHALE Got His Throat

For Jared and Ethan

Find out more about

Rudyard Kipling's
JUST so STORIES

at Shoo Rayner's fabulous website,

www.shoo-rayner.co.uk

First published in 2007 by Orchard Books
First paperback publication in 2008

ORCHARD BOOKS
338 Euston Road, London NW1 3BH
Orchard Books Australia
Level 17/207 Kent St, Sydney, NSW 2000

ISBN 978 1 84616 399 9 (hardback)
ISBN 978 1 84616 408 8 (paperback)

A CIP catalogue record for this book is available from the British Library.

1 3 5 7 9 10 8 6 4 2 (hardback)
1 3 5 7 9 10 8 6 4 2 (paperback)

Printed in the UK by CPI Bookmarque, Croydon, CR0 4TD

Orchard Books is a division of Hachette Children's Books,
an Hachette Livre UK company.

www.orchardbooks.co.uk

He ate the starfish and the garfish,
and the crab and the dab, and the
plaice and the dace, and the skate
and his mate, and the mackerel and
the pickerel, and the really truly
twirly-whirly eel.

He swallowed every fish that he
could find, until there was only one
small fish left in
all the sea.

This small fish was a 'Stute Fish. He
swam a little behind the Whale's right
ear, to keep out of harm's way.

'Stute Fish

The 'Stute Fish was very clever.
He stuck his hat to the side of the whale,
so he didn't have to swim to keep up.

Nowadays, 'Stute Fish are called Remora.

The small 'Stute Fish
said in his small 'Stute voice,
"Noble and generous Whale –
have you ever tasted Man?"

"No," boomed the Whale.
"What does Man taste like?"

"Nice," said the small 'Stute Fish.
"Nice but nubbly."

"Then fetch me some!" roared the
Whale, beating the sea with his tail
until it frothed up like a bubble bath.

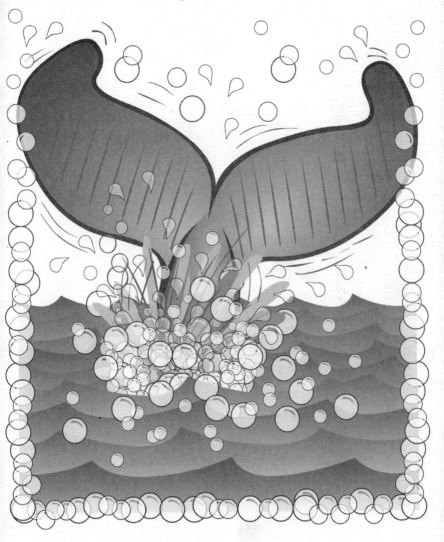

"One man at a time is quite enough,"
said the 'Stute Fish. "Now if you swim
to latitude Fifty North and longitude
Forty West, you will find, sitting
on a raft, in the middle of the sea,
a shipwrecked Sailor."

Latitude Fifty North and Longitude Forty West

The world is covered in imaginary lines and each one has a number.

Lines of latitude go round and round and lines of longitude go up and down.

Latitude Fifty North and longitude Forty West lies in the furthest middle of nowhere.

"What does he look like?" asked
the Whale.

"He is wearing a pair of blue shorts
held up with string," said the 'Stute
Fish. "And in his back pocket he has
a small, but very useful, penknife."

The Whale started swimming.

"But," continued the 'Stute Fish, "I think it's only fair to tell you that the Sailor is a man of infinite-resource-and-sagacity."

The Whale did not reply. He swam
and swam as fast as he could swim.

When he came to latitude Fifty North, longitude Forty West, he found the shipwrecked Sailor, sitting on a raft in the middle of the sea, just as the 'Stute Fish had said.

The Sailor was wearing a pair of blue shorts held up with string and in his back pocket he had a small, but very useful, penknife.

The Whale opened his mouth
back and back and back till it
nearly touched his tail.

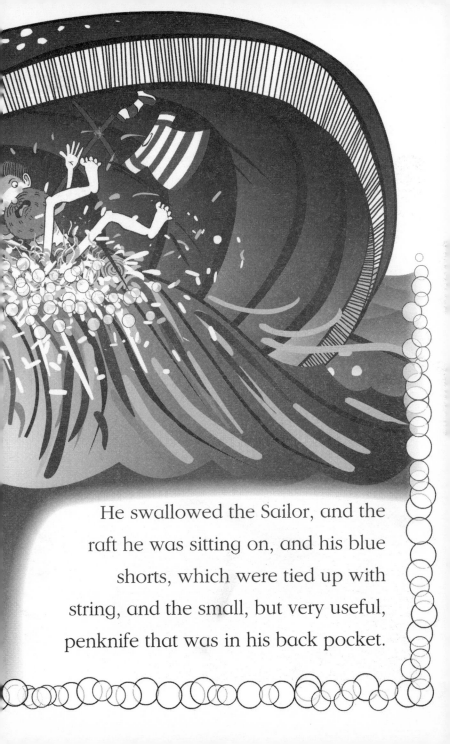

He swallowed the Sailor, and the
raft he was sitting on, and his blue
shorts, which were tied up with
string, and the small, but very useful,
penknife that was in his back pocket.

He swallowed them all down into his
warm, dark, insides in one huge gulp.

Then he
smacked his
lips twice, and
turned round
three times
on his tail.

When the shipwrecked Sailor, who was a man of infinite-resource-and-sagacity, found himself inside the Whale, he stumped and he jumped and he thumped and he bumped.

And he pranced and he danced, and he banged and he clanged, and he hit and he bit, and he leapt and he crept, and he prowled and he howled, and he hopped and he dropped.

And he cried and he sighed, and
he crawled and he bawled, and he
danced the hornpipe on some very
tender places, which made the
Whale feel very unhappy indeed.

The Hornpipe

To the tune of something fishy:

Heel and toe
Cross and weave,
Jump until
The floor is shaking.

Take your partner
Take your leave,
Dance until
Your feet are aching.

The Whale said to the 'Stute
Fish, "This man is very nubbly.
He is making me hic–hiccup.
What shall I do?"

"Tell him to come out,"
said the 'Stute Fish.

So the Whale called down his
throat to the shipwrecked Sailor,

"Come out and behave yourself.
I've got the hic–hic–hiccups!"

"Not today!" said the Sailor. "Take me to the white cliffs and the sandy shore of the land where I was born and...I'll think about it." Then the Sailor began to dance more than ever.

"You had better listen to him," the 'Stute Fish said to the Whale. "I did warn you that he is a man of infinite-resource-and-sagacity."

Infinite-resource-and-sagacity

Infinite: without end

Resourceful: capable, clever

Sagacity: ability to make good judgements

So the Man was as clever as the 'Stute Fish, if not more! He could solve any problem that came along – often with the help of his small, but very useful, penknife.

So the Whale swam and swam and swam with his flippers and his tail, as fast as a whale with hiccups can swim.

At last they came to the white cliffs and the sandy shore of the land where the Sailor was born.

The Whale charged the surf and rushed halfway up the beach. He opened his mouth wide and wide and wider still.

Then he called down his throat to the Sailor.

"Here are the white cliffs and the sandy shore of the land where you were born. Now come out and let me stop this hiccupping."

Just as he said sandy shore, the Sailor walked out of the Whale's mouth.

Now, all the time the Whale had been swimming, the Sailor had been hard at work. (Remember, he was a person of infinite-resource-and-sagacity.)

With his small, but very useful, penknife, he had cut up the raft and made it into a neat, square, criss-cross grating.

He tied it firm with the string that had held up his shorts, and he jammed that grating good and tight into the Whale's throat, and there it stuck!

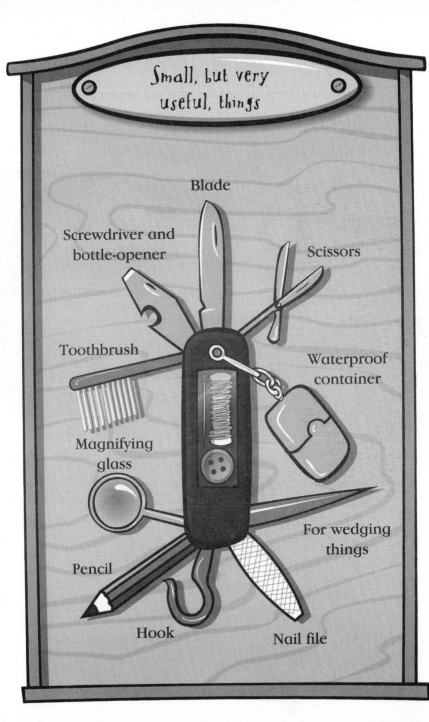

The Sailor stepped out onto the
sandy shore and spoke these words.
"By means of a grating,
I have stopped your ating."

(This was the
beginning of time,
remember, and poetry had
not really got started yet.)

The Sailor had used all the string that held up his shorts to tie the grating together.

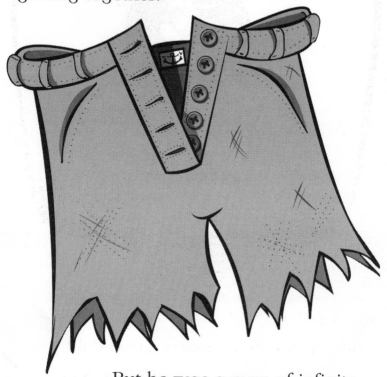

But he was a man of infinite-resource-and-sagacity, and his small penknife was more than very useful.

It had a hook with which the Sailor
pinned his shorts up nice and tight
– otherwise they would have fallen
down upon the sandy shore, for the
Sailor was thin from eating only dry
biscuit for three weeks.

The Sailor went home, got married and lived happily ever after, and so did the Whale.

But from that day on, the grating in the Whale's throat, which he could neither cough up nor swallow down, stopped him eating anything but very, very small fish.

And that is
the reason why
whales never eat
men or women or
little boys or girls.

The small 'Stute Fish went and hid
himself in the mud off the coast
of equatorial Africa. He was
afraid that the Whale
might be angry with
him. (Which he was!)

Rudyard Kipling's JUST SO STORIES

Retold and illustrated by

SHOO RAYNER

How the Whale Got His Throat	978 1 84616 408 8
How the Camel Got His Hump	978 1 84616 407 1
How the Leopard Got His Spots	978 1 84616 409 5
How the Rhinoceros Got His Skin	978 1 84616 410 1
The Beginning of the Armadilloes	978 1 84616 411 8
The Sing-Song of Old Man Kangaroo	978 1 84616 412 5
The Cat that Walked by Himself	978 1 84616 413 2
The Elephant's Child	978 1 84616 414 9

All priced at £3.99

Rudyard Kipling's Just So Stories are available from all good bookshops,
or can be ordered direct from
the publisher: Orchard Books, PO BOX 29, Douglas IM99 1BQ
Credit card orders please telephone 01624 836000
or fax 01624 837033 or visit our internet site: www.orchardbooks.co.uk
or e-mail: bookshop@enterprise.net for details.

To order please quote title, author and ISBN
and your full name and address.
Cheques and postal orders should be made payable to 'Bookpost plc.'
Postage and packing is FREE within the UK
(overseas customers should add £2.00 per book).

Prices and availability are subject to change.